T0067366

A Selection of Short Stories

by

Patricia Jean Alexander

authorHOUSE®

AuthorHouse™
1663 Liberty Drive
Bloomington, IN 47403
www.authorhouse.com
Phone: 1 (800) 839-8640

© 2005 Patricia Jean Alexander. All rights reserved.

No part of this book may be reproduced, stored in a retrieval system, or transmitted by any means without the written permission of the author.

Published by AuthorHouse 04/01/2020

ISBN: 978-1-4208-0537-6 (sc)
ISBN: 978-1-4634-7201-6 (e)

Print information available on the last page.

Any people depicted in stock imagery provided by Getty Images are models, and such images are being used for illustrative purposes only.
Certain stock imagery © Getty Images.

This book is printed on acid-free paper.

Because of the dynamic nature of the Internet, any web addresses or links contained in this book may have changed since publication and may no longer be valid. The views expressed in this work are solely those of the author and do not necessarily reflect the views of the publisher, and the publisher hereby disclaims any responsibility for them.

GIDDY-UP MOON
written/illustrated by
Patricia J. alexander

Once upon a time; there was a very delightful and an imaginative little boy named Demetrius Doone, he wanted to be a cowboy when he grew up, and he wanted to ride the moon. One evening after Demetrius and his Parents finished up with the wonderful meal that his mom made, that they agreed upon was really great,...

Demetrius noticed that the sun was going down, it was getting dark outside, his bedtime would be coming soon, it must be getting late. Demetrius and his Parents' decided to watch at least one movie, while they were sitting in their family room, on the big screen T.V.; mom made some Popcorn in the microwave, and dad made some lemonade flavored iced tea for every body. Demetrius noticed his father and mother looking at the grandfather clock, while he was... sitting on the carpeted floor which was against the wall, near the living room door, that was going tick-tock. Demetrius was told that it was time to go to bed, because it was already half-past eight, and we have a special day planned tomorrow, and we don't want to

Sleep too late! Demetrius was excited, because he loves his Parents, and he feels as though spending time together is always first-rate! Demetrius and his mom and dad walked up-stairs, as they normally do, hand-in-hand, to Demetrius's room, that is at the other end of the hall.

Before Demetrius goes to bed each night, he has to wash his
face, brush his teeth, Put on his favorite llama-Pajamas, and...

get on his knees, so that he can pray for his loved ones, his friends, and for others all throughout the land; this includes every girl and boy, every woman and man, according to God's divine grace.

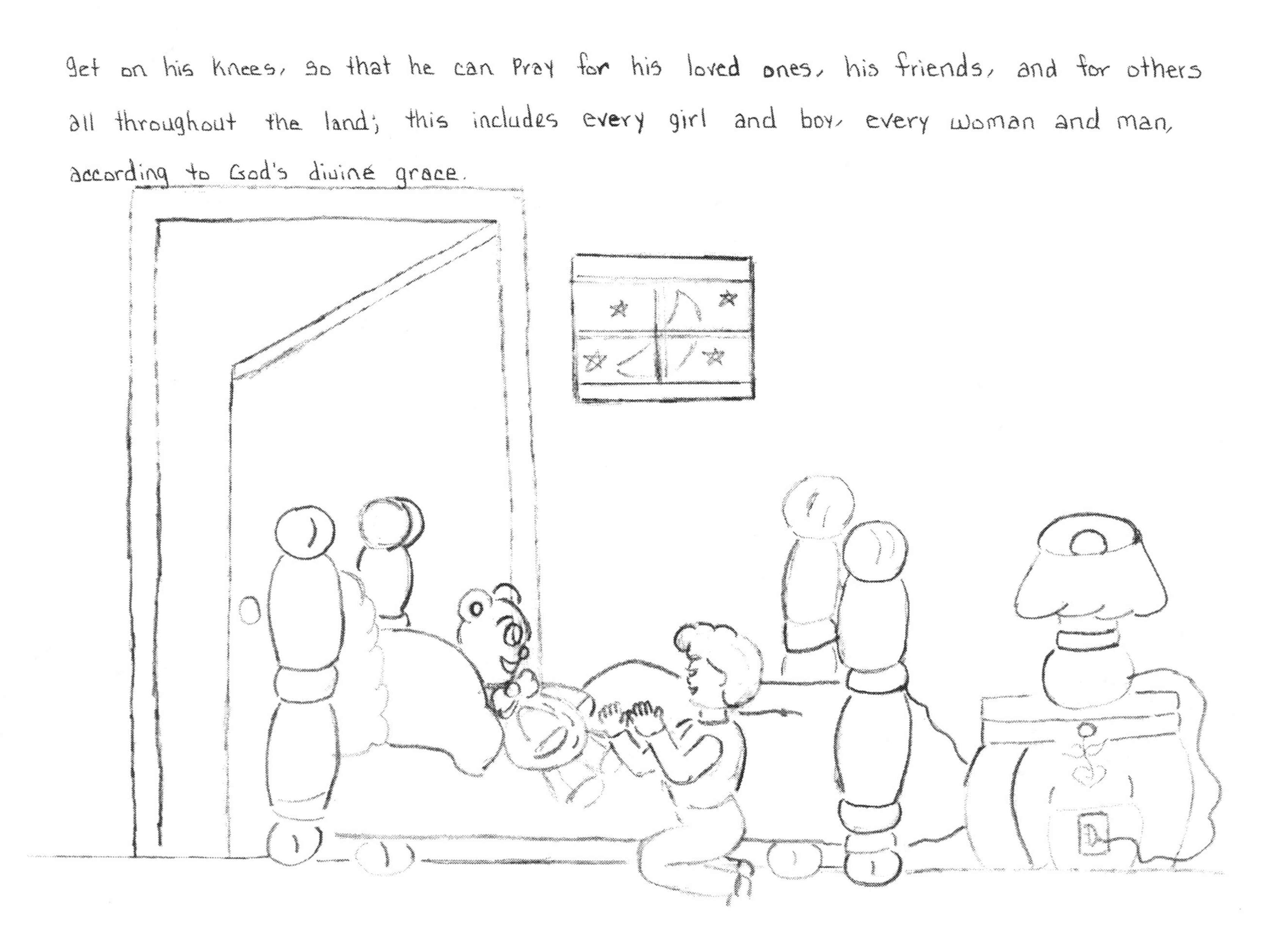

The Young lad's mom read two stories from his favorite books, while he was sitting on the bed, along with his dad, and his favorite teddy bear; she was sitting in a very comfortable rocking chair.

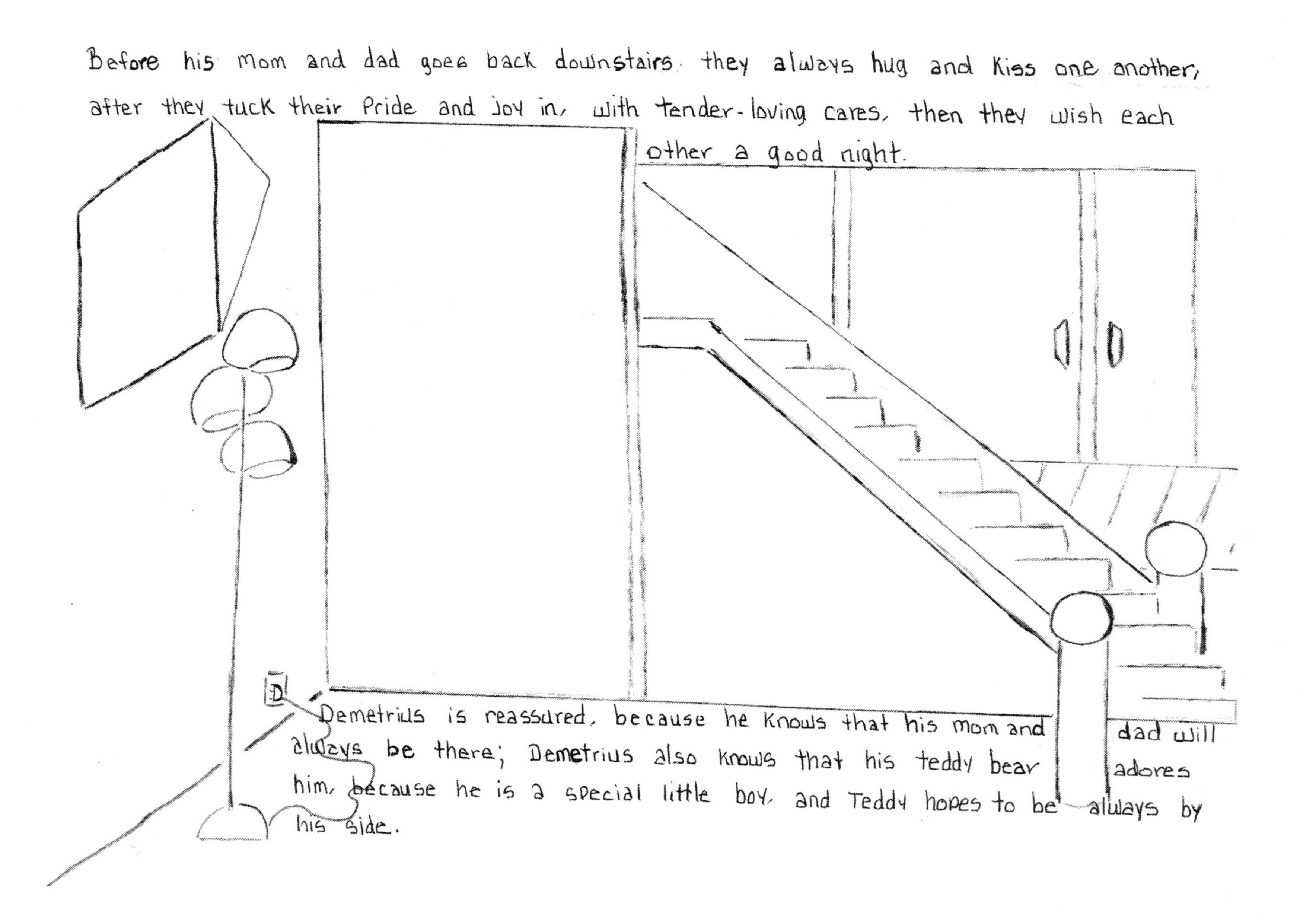

Before his mom and dad goes back downstairs. they always hug and Kiss one another, after they tuck their Pride and joy in, with tender-loving cares, then they wish each other a good night.

Demetrius is reassured, because he Knows that his mom and dad will always be there; Demetrius also Knows that his teddy bear adores him, because he is a special little boy, and Teddy hopes to be always by his side.

unfortunately, Demetrius could not fall asleep right away, because he had a lot of things on his mind; he began to think about the fun he had during the day. Demetrius tossed and he turned, he also noticed that his bedroom window was opened, why he even tried counting sheep. however, no matter what happened, he couldn't close his eyes.

Demetrius just laid there, as quietly as he possibly could, and then this wonderful idea came to him. He imagined himself lassoing the moon, so that he could take a spectacular ride, with his favorite teddy bear by his side, across the vast, cloudless sky. Their adventures gave the pair the opportunity to view Big Ben in London, England; the ancient relics of Italy, whose capitol city is Rome. And they were able to see the volcanoes of Waikiki, Hawaii, before they decided to go home.

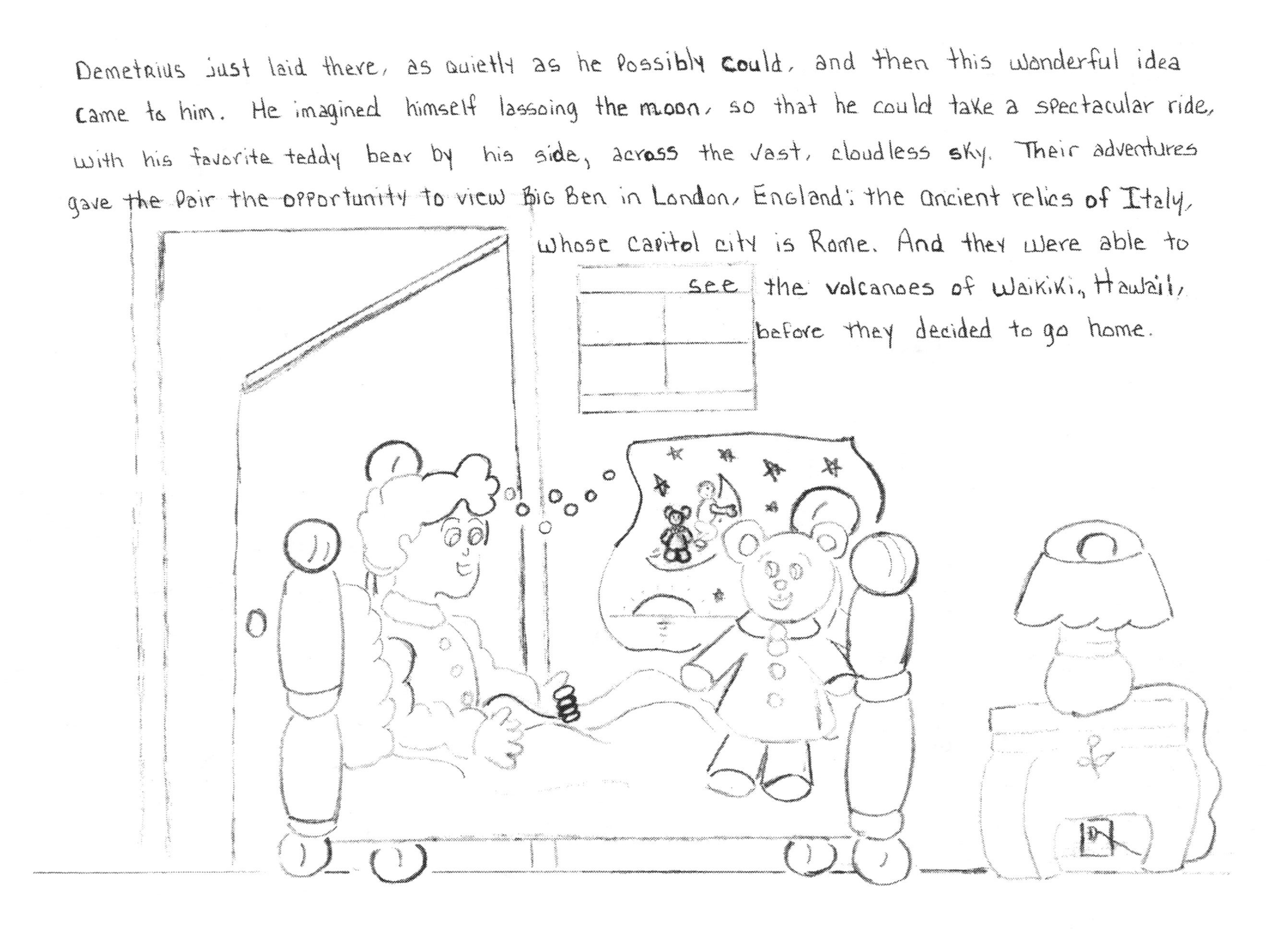

Before long, Demetrius grew tired, Teddy was getting tired as well, they began to rub their eyes and yawn. Demetrius knew that it would be another day coming, soon it would be dawn. Old Sol will be ready to come out to play; the sun will be ready to rise soon! Besides, Giddy-up MOON, we all had fun, however, you have to be fair, a part of the day with Old Sol, you will have to share.

I know that I can depend on you to do what is right; Thank you Giddy-up Moon for the wonderful ride! I hope that you will have a good night; Perhaps Teddy and I can come to visit with you again real real soon...
I love you Giddy-up Moon!
The End

Why Are You Crying; Why Do You Whine?
You Are A Good Little Porcupine!
Written & Illustrated by Patricia J. Alexander
Coloring Book

This is a story about a very little Porcupine, whose name is Tip-Top, that lives in the deep Part of the forest, with his father, Pop-Pop, his sister, Caroline, his mother, Clementine, and his brother, Be-bop.

The little Porcupine loves his family very much, and he has a lot of very, very
dear friends, that he plays with every day...

that he likes to spend
time with, who live on
the other side of...
Critter Creek Bends

One Saturday morning, after breakfast was served, Tip-Top's father, mother, sister, and his brother worked hard, in order to finish their chores. The Porcupine family's normal routine is to load up into the family car, so that they can drive into the nearest town, which is called Peaceful Shores.

Little Porcupine loves going for a ride with his family, but he does not like going to the store, and he does not care for shopping, or standing in the long grocery lines.

While Tip-Top's parents were taking care of their errands, Be-bop, Caroline, and the little Porcupine was allowed to ride on a mini-train; and they all got a brand new toy that included a kite, a ball, and a new airplane.

Clementine Porcupine bought our favorite ice cream. Pop-Pop purchased some frosting, along with some mix for a cake; Sunday is Caroline's birthday, and Be-bop just performed in his first school play; that was titled "Do Horses Sey neigh; Do They Eat Hey?"

It was still early when the little Porcupine and his family arrived home. Everyone helped out by carrying a bag into the house. even Tip-Top carried a can of paint, which was the color of seafoam. The little Porcupine wanted to take advantage of the wonderful weather they were having...

It was a beautiful Day; it was already the first Day of Spring, You See!

Little Porcupine liked being outside, and
he liked smelling the flowers, as well as
feeling the warm breezes on his face.

Tip-Top also liked Playing a Game of hide
and seeks; he also liked to hear the songs
that the birds sinG!

On this particular day, when Tip-Top was outside, he played a game of freeze tag, with his pals, that included a girl-squirrel named Sal, and a duck-billed platy-pus named Mattie. Sal the squirrel was chasing Tip-Top, Mattie, and the others around the cool-pool lake, when the little porcupine stopped to take a rest; because he was tired of running around, and he needed to take a quick break...

All of a sudden, the little Porcupine glanced at his reflection, which was in the cool-Pool lake, **then** the Porcupine got very upset, why he even began to **cry**; he even started to **whine**! Believe it or not; he had never seen himself before, and he was wondering what those pointy things were, that were going up and down his spine. All of the creatures that are close friends with Tip-Top, ran to see what was wrong with him, why even the birds stopped singing their songs!

The critters asked the little Porcupine;
why are you crying? why do you whine;
You are a Good little Porcupine! We love you Tip-Top
and we like being with you every day... We like it
when you come to Play; to us. You look just fine!
When Tip-Top heard the special words from his best
friends, he stopped whining, he no longer felt sad!

The little Porcupine felt Good about himself, he began to smile, every thing; once again, was all right! Tip-Top told his mother, father, sister, and his brother about how he discovered the way that he looks, while they were having dinner that night. Every one reassured the little Porcupine that they love him; they also feel that he is very special to them...

Tip-Top will always have a Place in their hearts; they will never Part! The little Porcupine said hopefully: "I will always be there for my loved ones, and they will always be mine after all, I am a Good little Porcupine!"

The End

Powder The Goldfish

Written/illustrated by Patricia J. alexander

D is for Don't
T is for Trust
H is for Humans

Powder the Puffy Faced Goldfish

Written and Illustrated by Patricia Jean Alexander

Once upon a time there was a wonderful family of goldfish, which owned a lovely home, a big screen T.V., and a bold-wish satellite dish.

The family included a father, a mother, and an older sister, along with her younger brother, a grandfather, and a grandmother. they were very caring, and they all loved each other!

Grandpa and father works at the Old English Furniture Polish Factory, every day, five days a week, while grandma and mother stay at home, in order to cook and clean, while they watch their favorite Mr. Bubble soap-opera story.

On the weekends, Powder and his sister like to get together with their friends, in order to play a game of hide and seek near the sea foam slope, and to listen to music, under the Grey Dome Peak.

Powder the puffy-faced goldfish likes to carry his own lunch with him to a place that is named the Pearl Fountain Grade School, in his favorite shark skin back pack. Trish, Powder's older sister goes to the Swirl Mountain High School, which has its very own mermaid pool.

Either mother or grandma always makes the little goldfish his favorite treat that he loves to eat! Powder enjoys having a sandwich that is made with smooth, creamy peanut butter and berry flavored jellyfish, this makes his meal so tasty and sweet.

The little goldfish washes his lunch down with a cold glass of seaweed milk, to him, this is the best deal, and he thinks this is really neat! Mother or grandma prepares breakfast for the children each day; and they always take the time to hug, kiss and say good bye, before they are off on their merry way.

After a day at work for grandpa and father, a full day of housework and cooking for grandma and mother, along with a day of school for Powder and Trish, every one likes to sit down to the table, in order to enjoy a family-style dinner.

While the goldfish family is eating their meal, they usually talk about the events of the day, this is always a winner! Before the children go to the bed at night, they are allowed to have a healthy snack that is very light.

Finally, Powder knows that as long as he is a good little goldfish, his mother or his grandmother will always make his favorite lunch for him, he will always get his wish!

The End

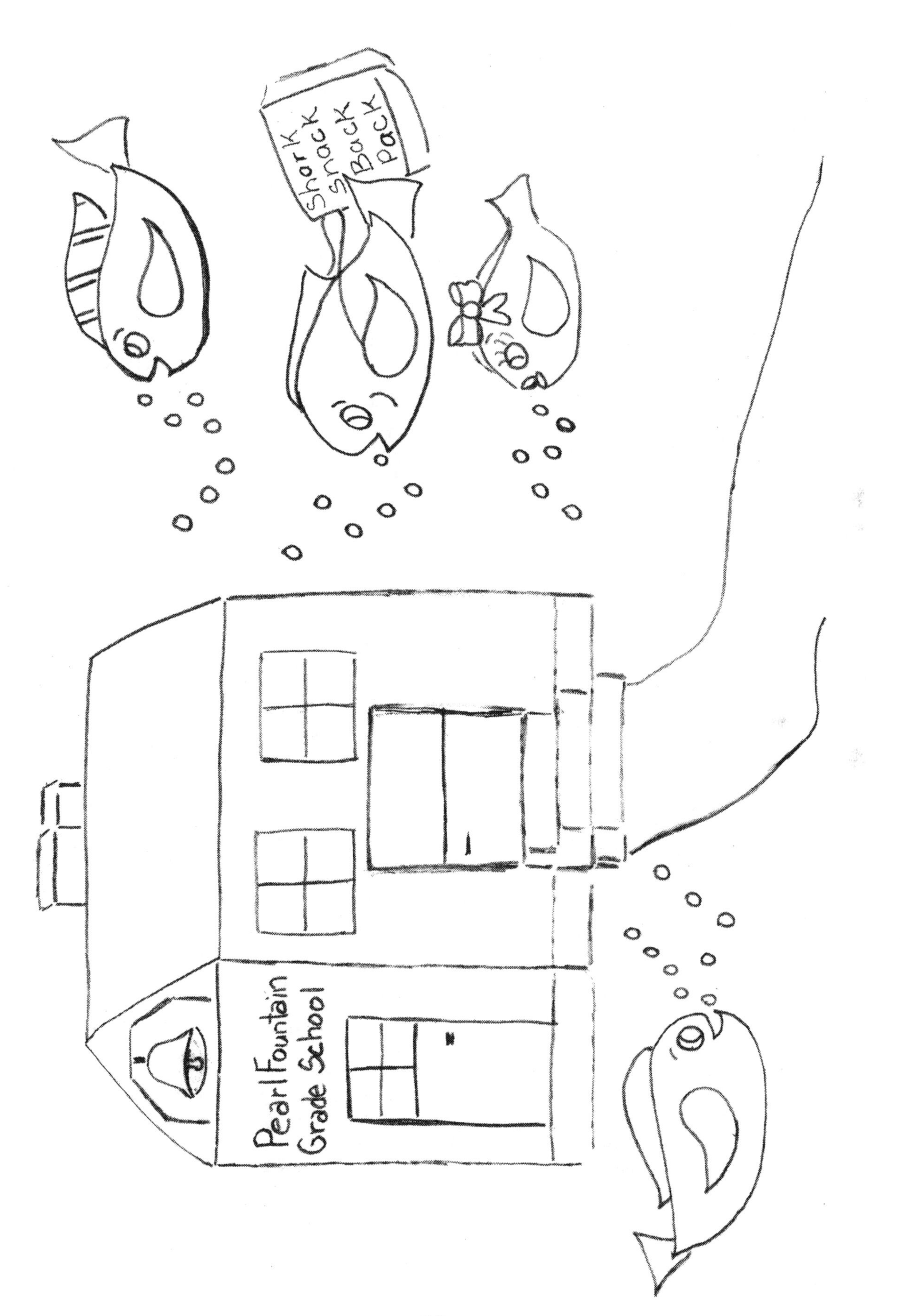
Shark Snack Back Pack
Pearl Fountain Grade School

Harry's New Hat

Written and Illustrated by
Patricia Jean Alexander

This is a hilarious story about a hippotamus named Harry; he lives on a tame, Game Preserve in Newberry. Harry has an older sister named Sherry, and a younger brother named Garry. Harry's father's name is Larry, and his mother's name is Mary.

One day Harry came up with the notion
to visit with his family that lives
across the ocean;
he was all prepared
to leave, but he
couldn't find his
hat, or his fine
Jacket that
has a patch on each sleeve.

It seems as though the hippo misplaced the derby that has a feather,
he searched high and low; Harry doesn't like to roam about,
without it.

Harry the hippo loves to dress up in fancy clothes, he always wears a hat. He wears it where ever he goes, can you imagine that? Harry has a friend that is a toucan, his name is Gerald Gus. Every one calls him Jerry for short.
Gerald Gus can be seen riding on the back of the hippotomus, when ever Harry decides to stroll along the plains that are flat. Harry is such a good sport. Jerry prefers being with the hippo, instead of getting on the bus, no matter what the weather is like out side, even when it rains!

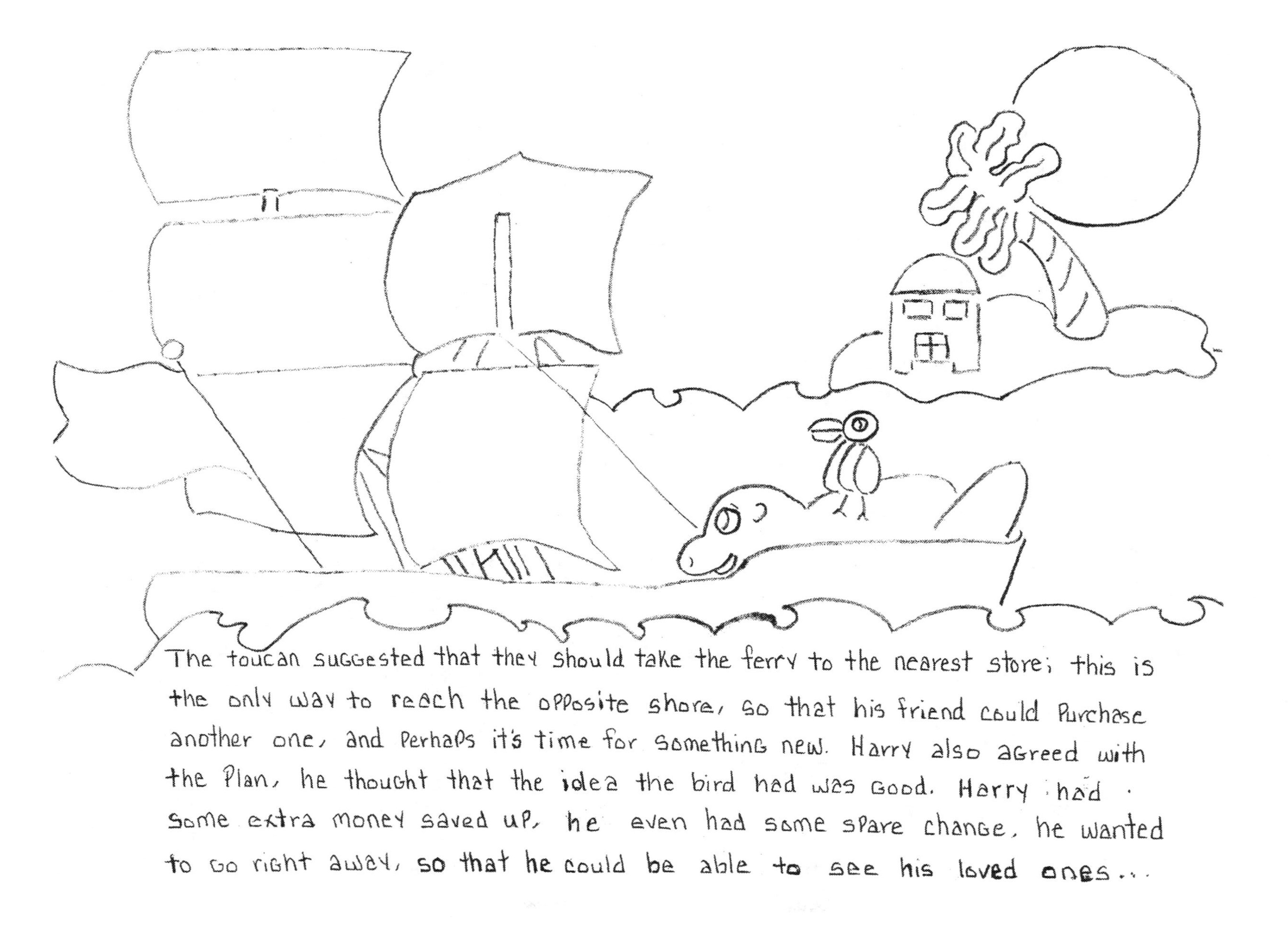
The toucan suggested that they should take the ferry to the nearest store; this is the only way to reach the opposite shore, so that his friend could purchase another one, and perhaps it's time for something new. Harry also agreed with the plan, he thought that the idea the bird had was good. Harry had some extra money saved up, he even had some spare change, he wanted to go right away, so that he could be able to see his loved ones...

before the end of the day. Jerry and Harry encountered an ordeal that was very, very strange, when they got off of the happy-hippo ferry, once they arrived to the other side of the island.

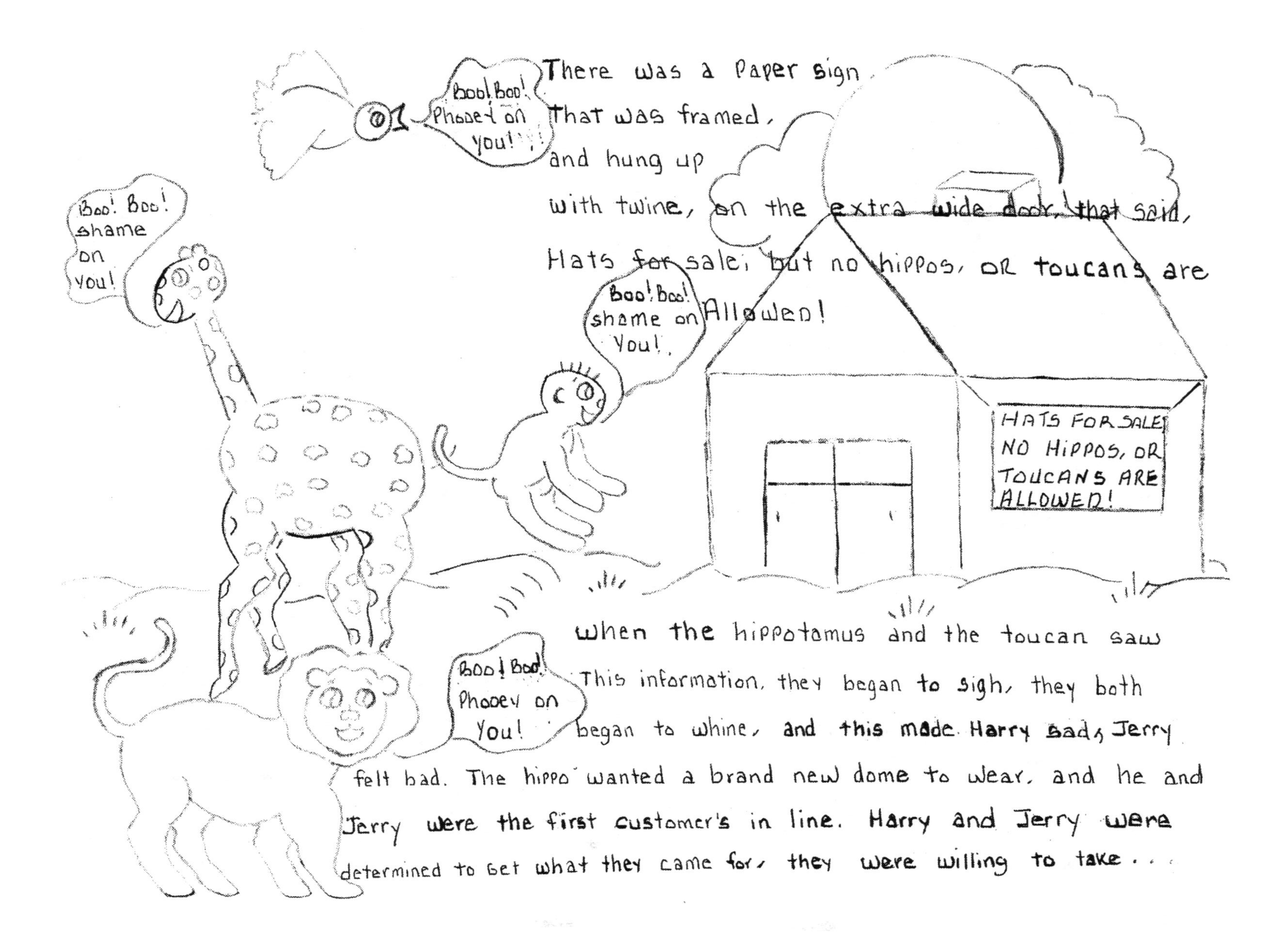
Boo! Boo! Phooey on you!
There was a Paper sign
That was framed,
and hung up
with twine, on the extra wide door, that said,
Hats for sale, but no hippos, or toucans are
Allowed!
Boo! Boo! shame on You!
Boo! Boo! shame on You!
HATS FOR SALE NO HIPPOS, OR TOUCANS ARE ALLOWED!
Boo! Boo! Phooey on You!
when the hippotamus and the toucan saw
This information, they began to sigh, they both
began to whine, and this made Harry sad, Jerry
felt bad. The hippo wanted a brand new dome to wear, and he and
Jerry were the first customer's in line. Harry and Jerry were
determined to get what they came for, they were willing to take . . .

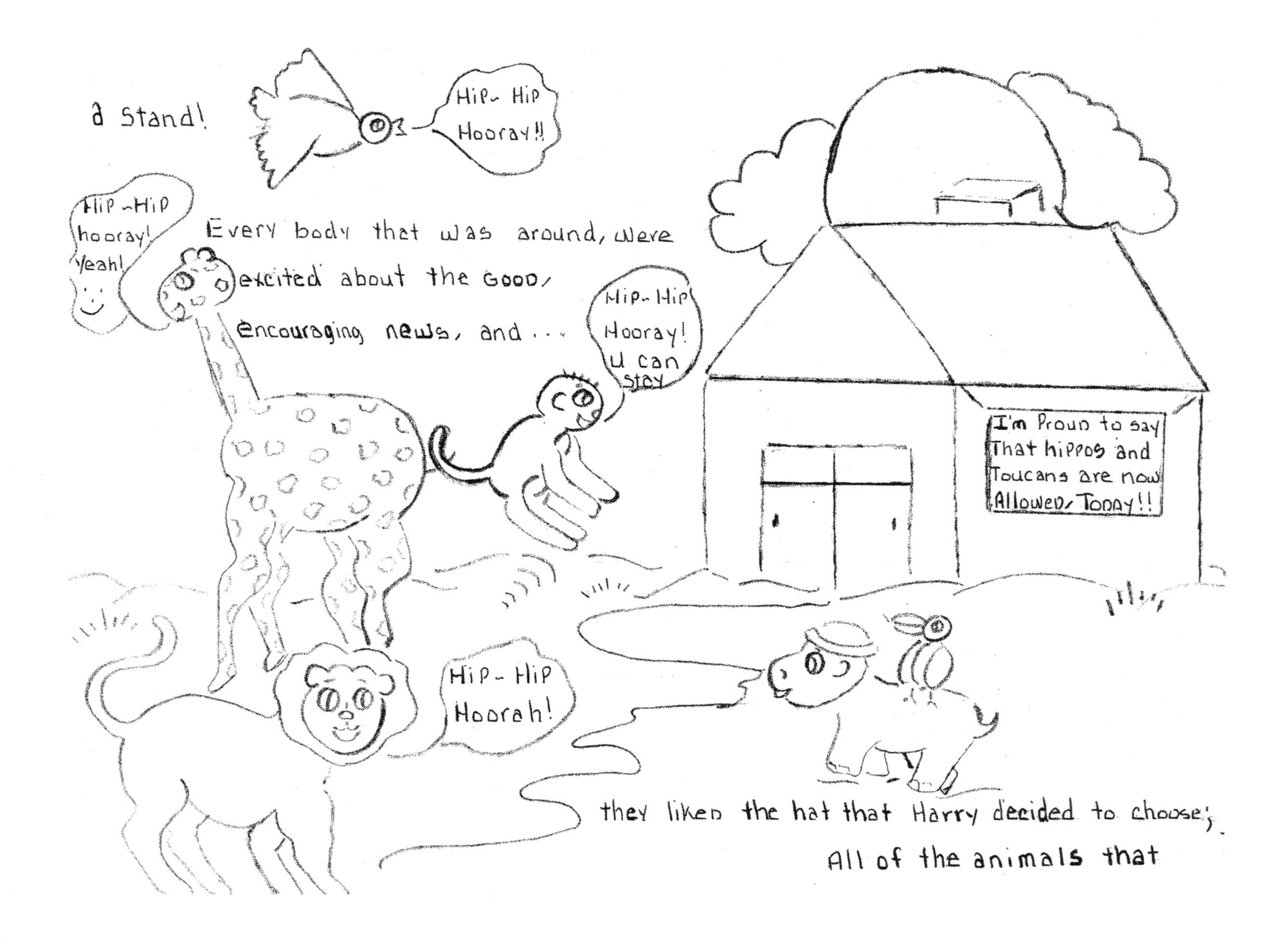
a Stand!
Hip- Hip Hooray!!
Hip -Hip hooray! Yeah!
Every body that was around, Were excited about the GOOD, encouraging news, and . . .
Hip- Hip Hooray! U can stay
I'm Proud to say That hippos and Toucans are now Allowed, Today!!
Hip- Hip Hoorah!
they liked the hat that Harry decided to choose;.
All of the animals that

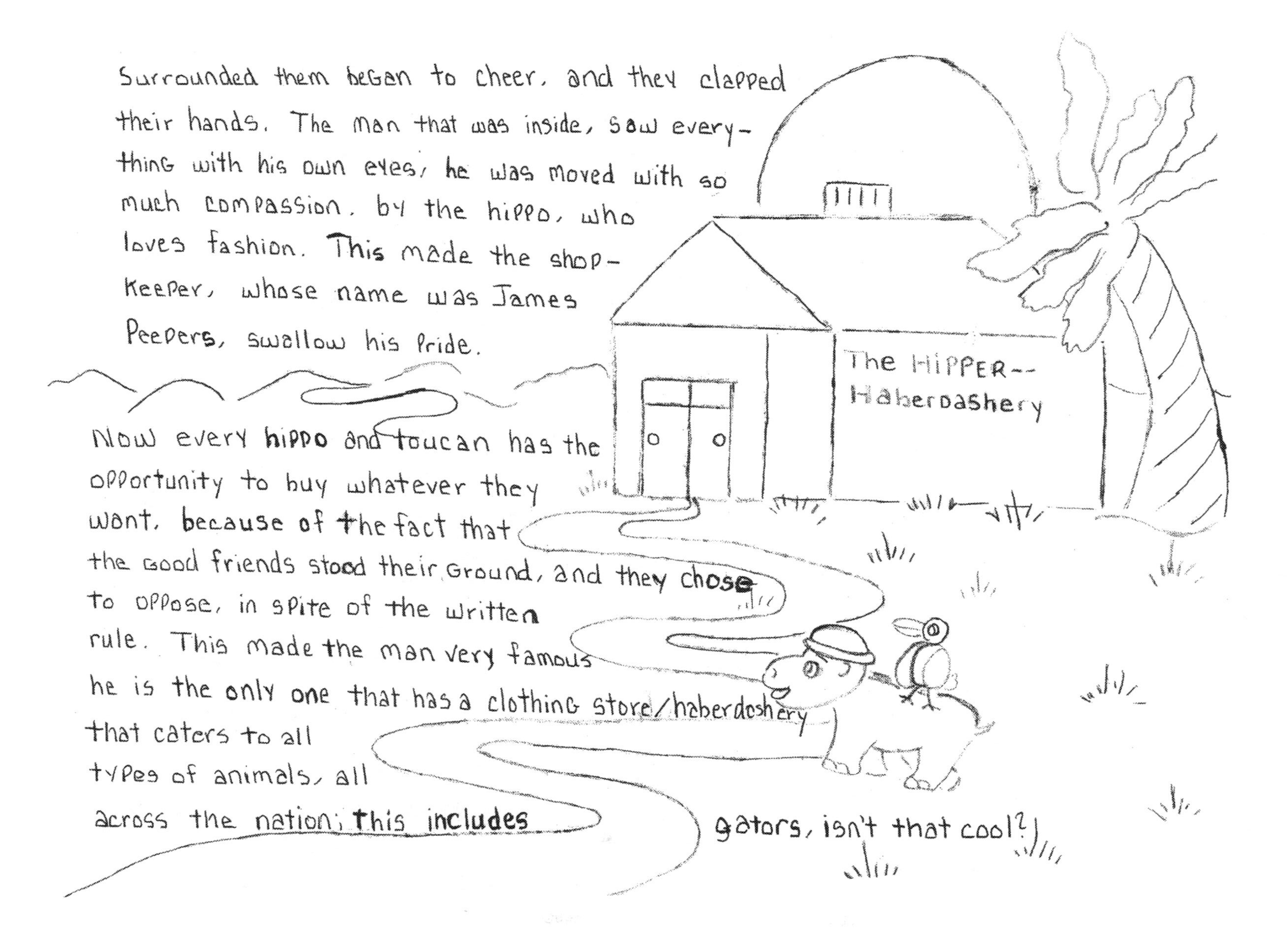

Surrounded them began to cheer, and they clapped their hands. The man that was inside, saw everything with his own eyes; he was moved with so much compassion, by the hippo, who loves fashion. This made the shopkeeper, whose name was James Peepers, swallow his pride.

Now every **hippo** and toucan has the opportunity to buy whatever they want, **because of the** fact that the good friends stood their ground, and they **chose** to oppose, in spite of the written rule. This made the man very famous he is the **only one** that has a clothing store/haberdashery that caters to all types of animals, all across the nation; **This includes** gators, isn't that cool?

The kind owner of the shop had all kinds of hats for sale. Some were made of suede and leather; some were brown and some were blue. All of the hats were on display, either on the table, or hanging on a rack, he even had some in a stack, in the back. Harry found the perfect hat, he liked it really well. Jerry and the owner liked the choice that the hippo made, and they thought that he looked swell.

Harry arrived at his Parent's home, before it was too late. The hippo's family adores him; they think that he looked quite handsome. Harry had some money left over, so he bought a gift for his mother and father, and he gave his sister and brother a pack of chewing gum, and some Grand, Purple, and Green Plums.

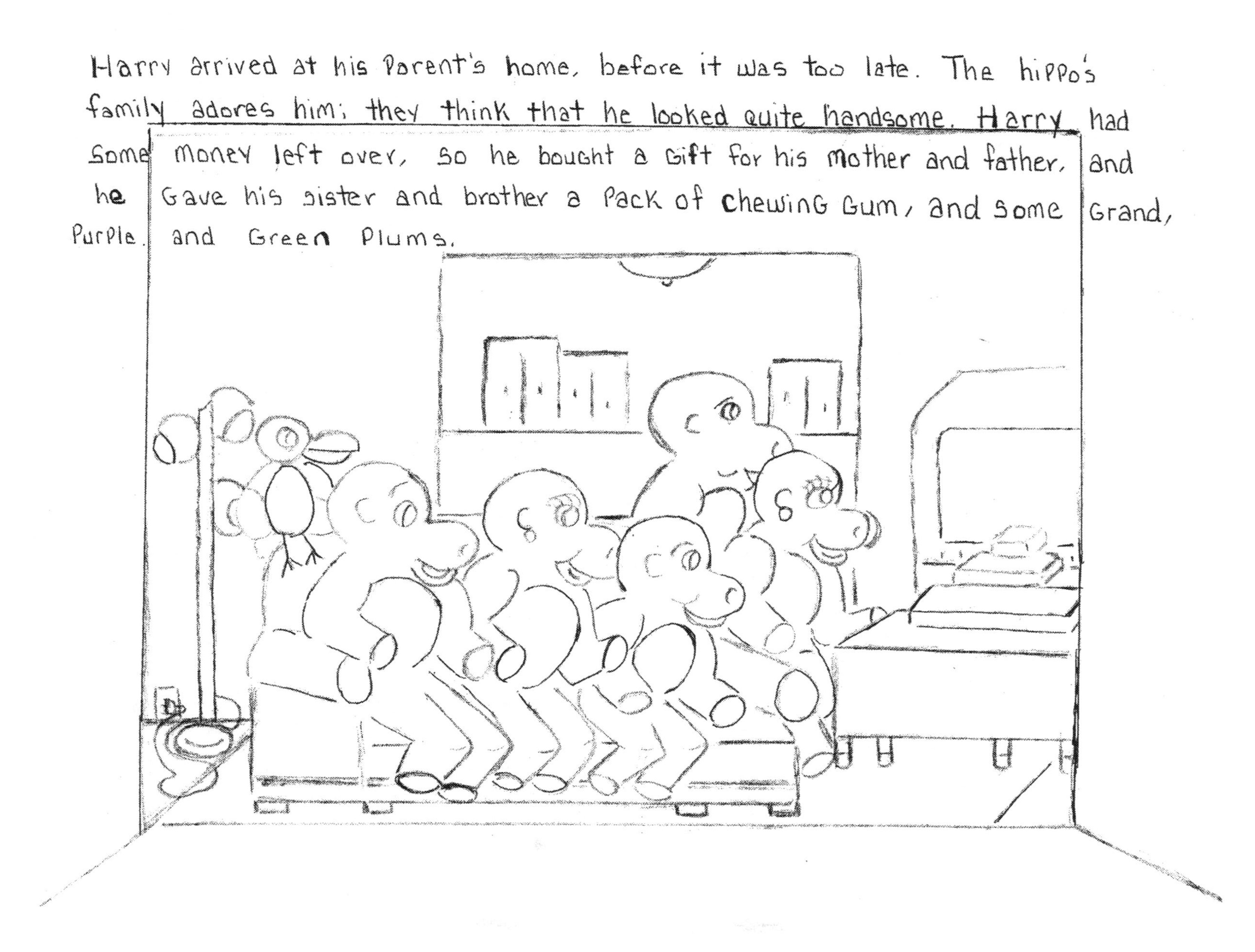

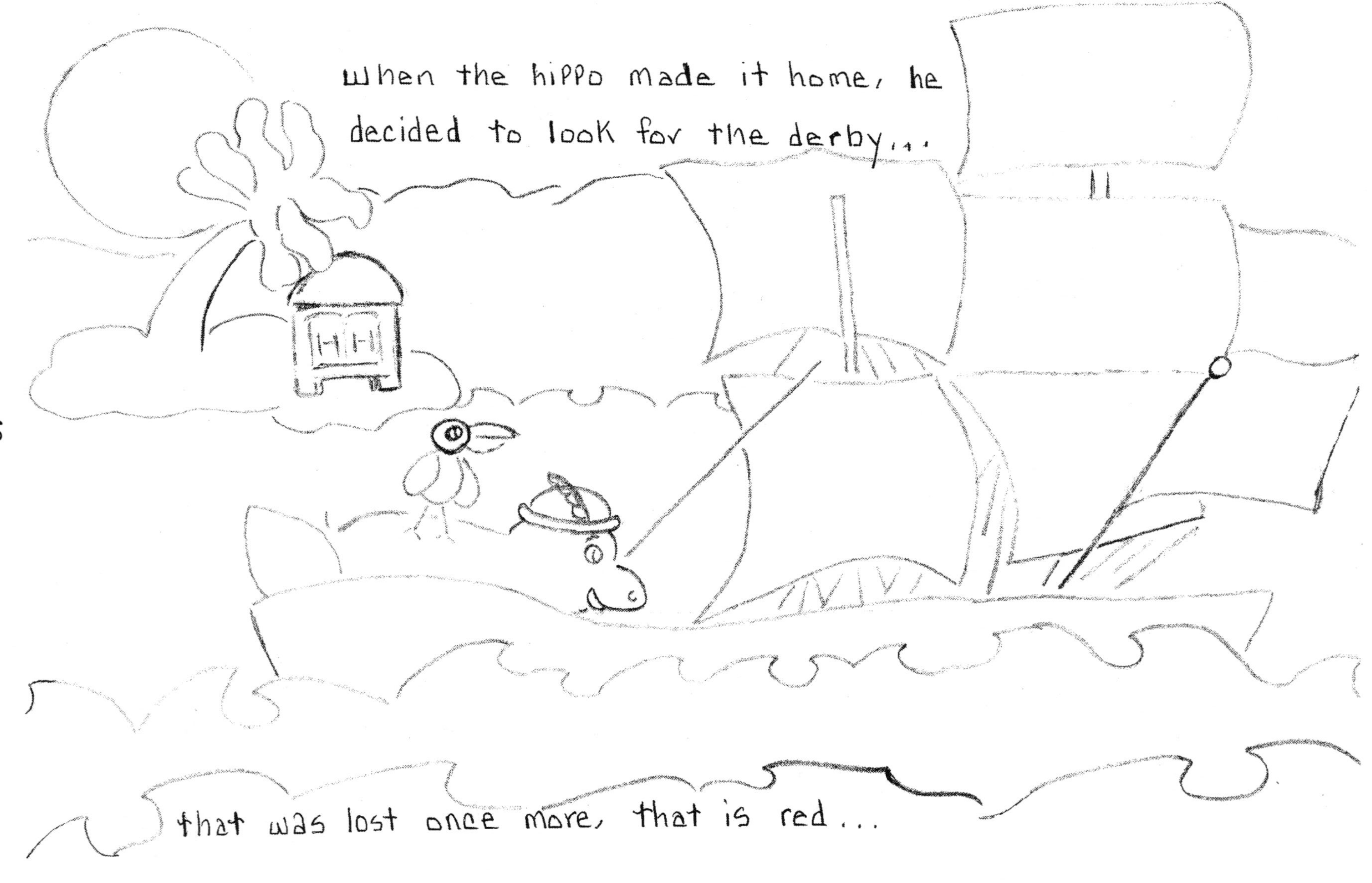
when the hippo made it home, he
decided to look for the derby...
that was lost once more, that is red...

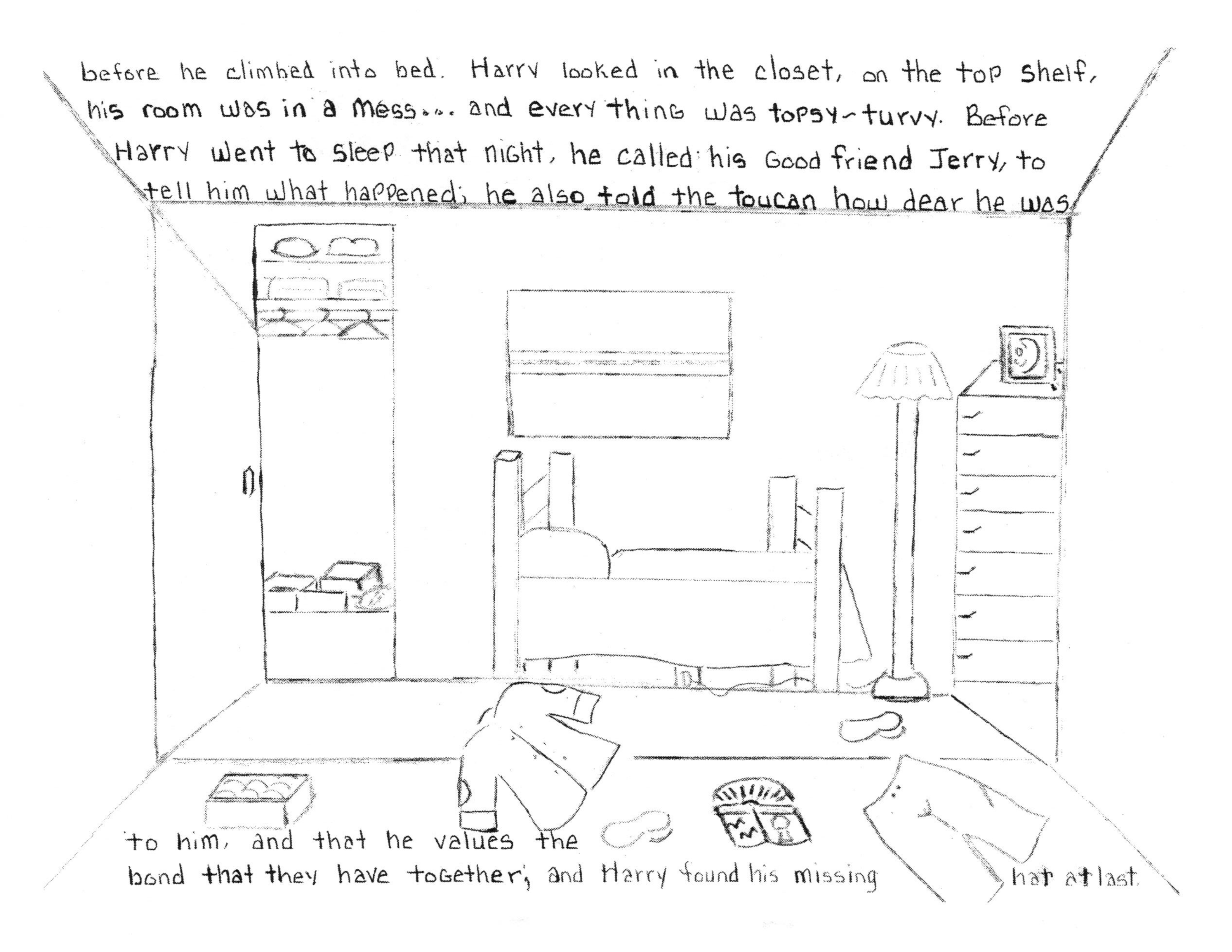
before he climbed into bed. Harry looked in the closet, on the top shelf,
his room was in a mess... and every thing was topsy-turvy. Before
Harry went to sleep that night, he called his Good friend Jerry, to
tell him what happened; he also told the toucan how dear he was
to him, and that he values the
bond that they have together; and Harry found his missing
hat at last.

The hippo feels as though friendship is much more
than any hat, no
matter what
it might cost!
Jerry, having a pal like you, makes me proud! If you
like, let's go for a swim on tomorrow. Jerry said that
he would love to go for a nice dip, as long as Harry has
a swimming cap that he can borrow.

The Mayor of Newberry has
also arranged to have an annual
celebration, on behalf of Harry
the hippo, and Jerry the toucan's
dedication. An ice cream social
is held in the first booth, that's
set up at the Bayer County
Fair.

The Manual Senior High School Marching Band was Picked to Perform in a Parade, in order to honor the brave Pair. The Group is quite talented, they play such, lovely, wonderful music.

This is how the students received their fame, along with their bandleader, Mr. Ray Dusic.

The hippo and the toucan signed up so that they can participate in the potato sack races.
Harry and Jerry won; because all of the other contestants slipped and fell on their faces. Why one of them even broke his front tooth; isn't that awful, isn't that a shame?
Start
Trying to win a teddy bear is not always an easy game
Finish Line!
PotatoSack Races held today!

Welcome to
the Baker
County Fair
come in and
WIN A
TEDDY
Bear

Harry loves hot fudge sundae's, and Jerry likes waffle cones, that is topped with a dreamy, sweet treat, that is loaded with blueberries and pecans.

Occasionally, Harry and Jerry likes to have their favorite desserts under the branches and leaves of a huge shade tree.

If the carnival is a success, sometimes the festivities can be carried over until Monday. I enjoy going to the carnival; I love to win prizes, like the real big Teddy bears.
I like to ride the roller coasters, especially the ones that are tall and curvy. Once again Harry was at peace within himself. As long as Harry wears his hat, you will be able to spot him in a crowd!
The End

Shamrock: The Polar Bear Prince

Once upon a time, there was a Polar bear Prince that lived in a Place that is called forth Ham Hock. The city is located in the northern hemisphere of Alaska.

Shamrock the Polar bear Prince inhabits this area of the land with some
Eskimos, some Penguins, some dogs that are huskies, Some fish that
are muskies, and some animals that are not warm blooded mammals.

The Polar bear Prince had a dad that was sixty years old, and his mom was fifty-five. Shamrock's Parent's were very rich; but thrifty.
He also has a brother named Molar, a brother named Jamal, and a sister named Michelle,... as well, they are still alive.

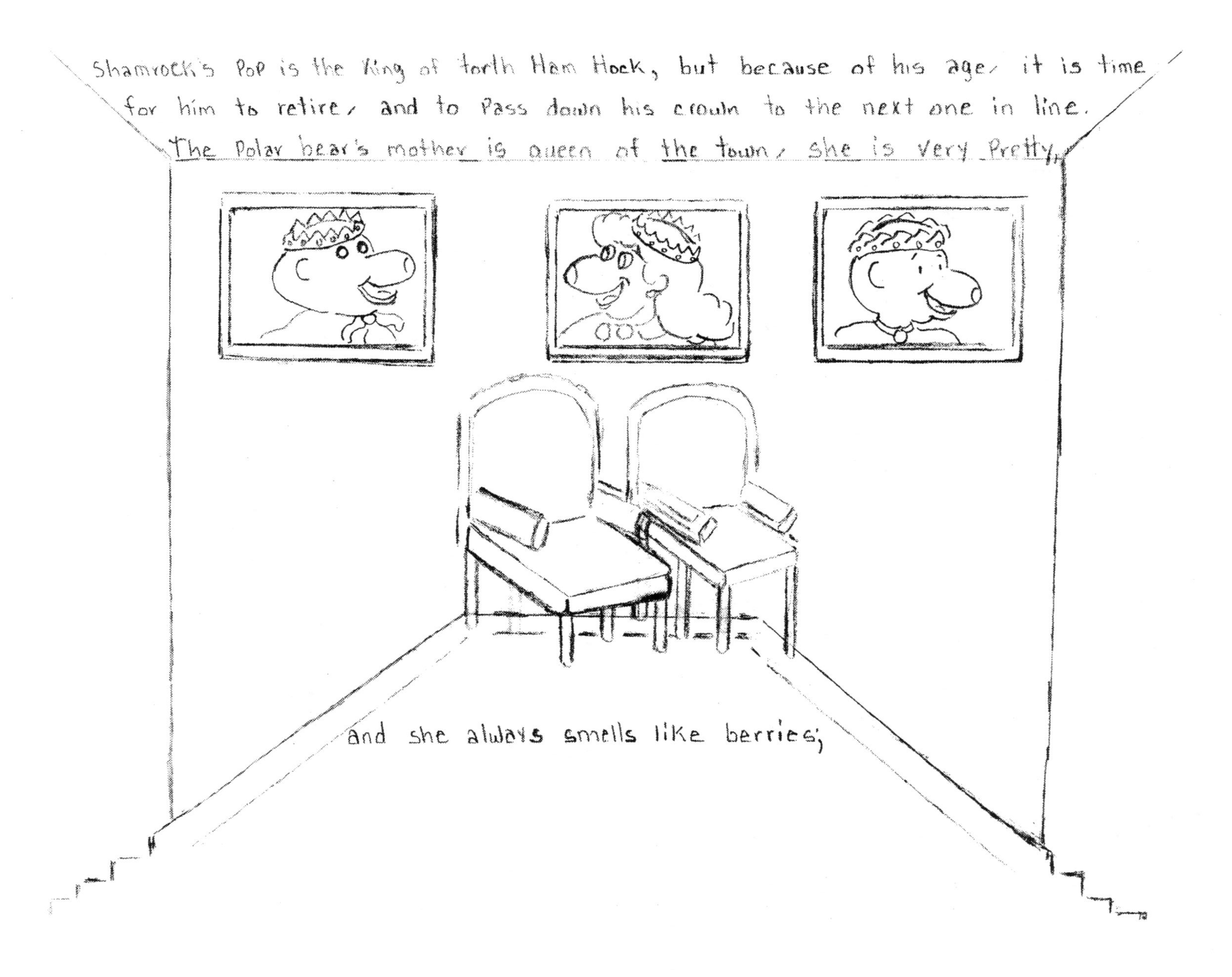
Shamrock's Pop is the King of torth Ham Hock, but because of his age, it is time
for him to retire, and to Pass down his crown to the next one in line.
The Polar bear's mother is queen of the town, she is very Pretty,
and she always smells like berries;

they thrive on nuts, ice water and cherries.
ICE WATER
ICE WATER
ICE WATER
walnut
Dad and mom loves their son's, and their daughter, and they live next door to
a family of otter's, whose last name is Potter.

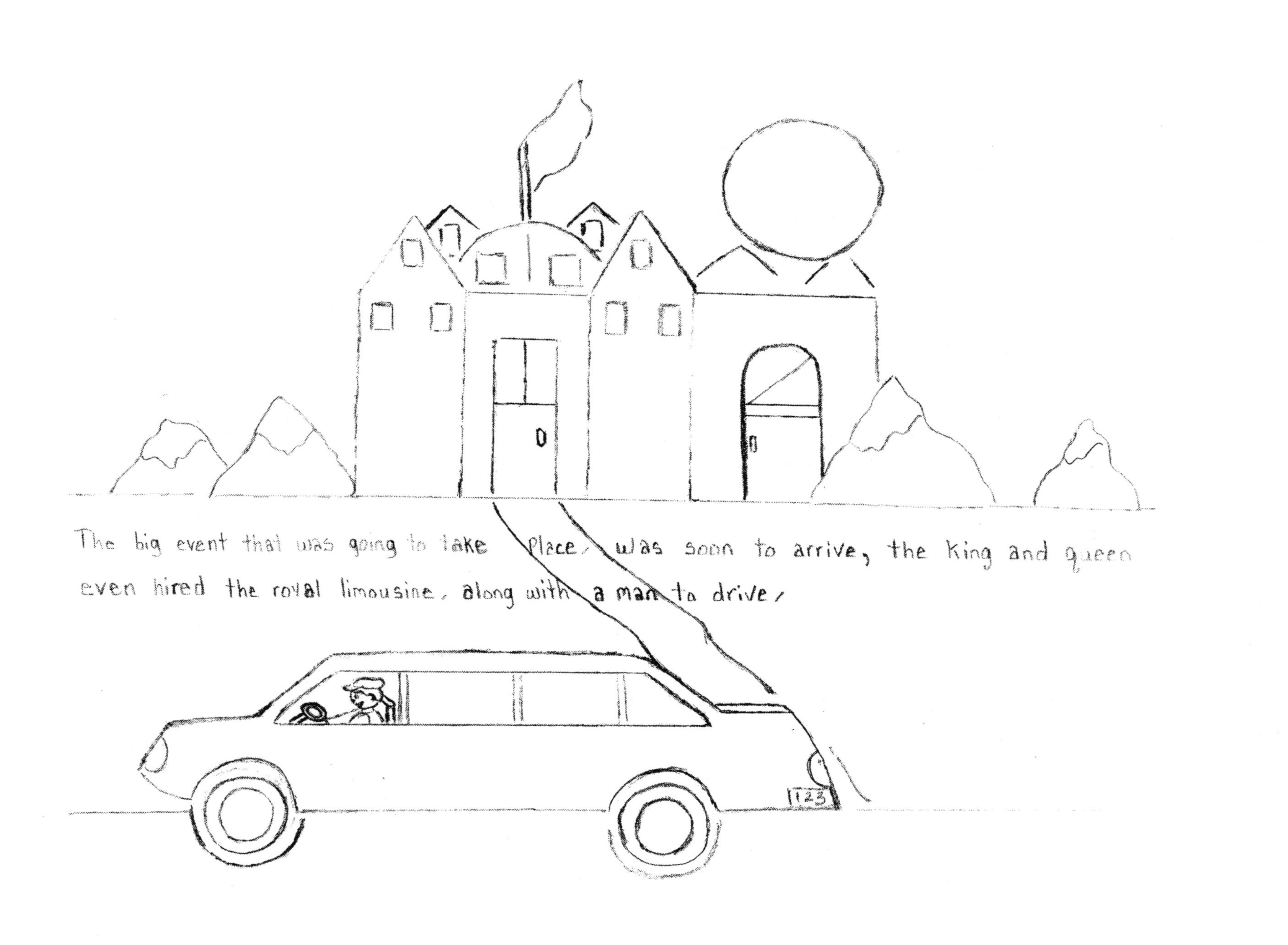
The big event that was going to take place, was soon to arrive, the King and queen
even hired the royal limousine, along with a man to drive,
123

and they hired some caterer's to prepare and bring the cuisine,

and some prime, fine wine.

One of the server's accidentally wasted some of the wine on Shamrock, before it could be tasted; it made the Polar bear feel sad, everyone that was present felt bad, his mom and dad flew into a rage, because some of the wine spilled on to the floor.

The wine turned his fur a purplish/blue; The waitress, whose name was Bess, made such a mess! She cried as she ran out of the door.

Shamrock was full of embarrassment, mental anguish, shame and pain; he

didn't know what to do, the Polar bear Prince didn't have a clue!
molar, Jamal and Michelle told their brother not to be so afraid,
RAIN WATER
SOAP
and they told him not to give up on hope yet; you will be ok; that is
not a Permanent dye, we came up with an idea; we will get rid of the...

terrible stain with some soap, along with the pure drops of the fallen rain, so don't you worry, don't you fret!

The solution that Shamrock's brothers and sister used worked like a charm, why it even cleared up the stain that was on his arm. It's a good thing that his fur turned back to its original color, along with soap, and a good rinse, that includes his skin. Thankfully, the wine didn't do any serious harm.

Shamrock received his crown, he became king according to plan, just as his dad
and Mom wished for, and all of their neighbors and friends
attended the ball and celebration.
hurray!
hurray!...
The former Polar bear Prince vowed to
rule well, with true dedication;

every body enjoyed the meat, the sweets, and the music; every one ate heartily, it was quite a swell Party!

The newly crowned King even Participated in the festivities, why he was even
allowed to dance with a polar bear Princess named Chance, in the Wet
Camel Ballroom, and he began to sing.

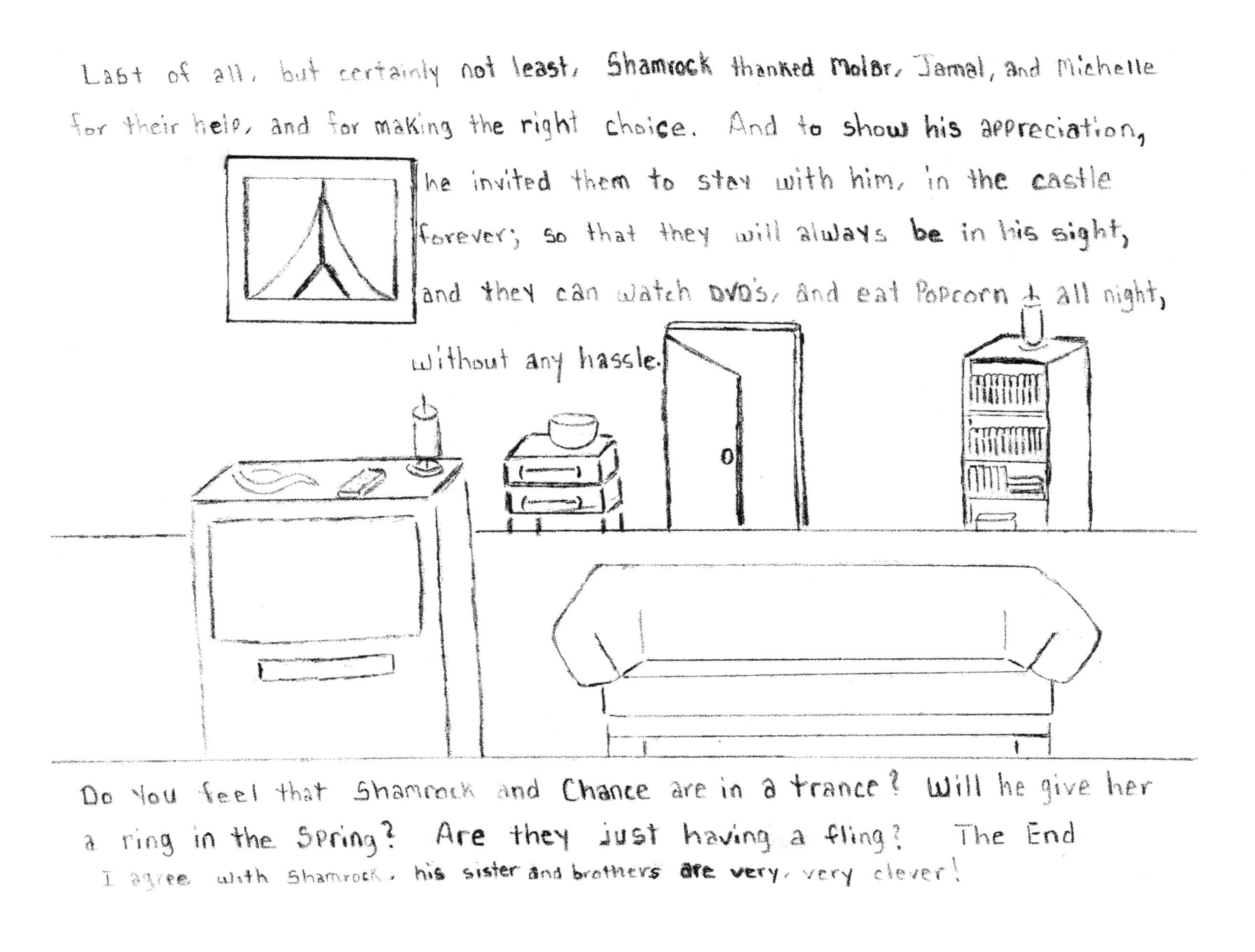
Last of all, but certainly not least, Shamrock thanked Molar, Jamal, and Michelle
for their help, and for making the right choice. And to show his appreciation,
he invited them to stay with him, in the castle
forever; so that they will always be in his sight,
and they can watch DVD's, and eat Popcorn + all night,
without any hassle.
Do You feel that Shamrock and Chance are in a trance? Will he give her
a ring in the Spring? Are they just having a fling? The End
I agree with Shamrock, his sister and brothers are very, very clever!

The Hummingbird that Couldn't...
written/illustrated by Patricia Jean Alexander

Once upon a time, there was a small hummingbird that lived in a Place that is called, the forest of Dunce Hall. The hummingbird's name is Fair Grace; she has a lot of friends, sometimes...

Welcome to
The Forest of
Dunce Hall

they like to play a game of bare mat space ball. Grace and her buddies are
very social creatures, on the ground, and in the air; why they even care
for fuddy-duddies, every where!

unfortunately, Fair Grace had a serious Problem; this hummingbird was not like the other ones at all. Grace does not have the ability to hum, sing, or make a sound; she can't even carry a tune, with the utility of a cruddy spoon.

The hummingbird decided to seek more guidance from some body, because she was ashamed of her situation; and she was feeling quite insecure. Fair Grace hoped that some one would be able to cure her for sure; she was becoming impatient.

One of her neighbors that stays next door
heard of the hummingbird's Poor
dilemma; the animal is a
fox; her name is Miss Emma.
The fox told Grace about a man
that is a wizard, he lives on the
other end of the forest, with his
brother, whose name is Edwin Word.

Miss Emma said "Perhaps he knows a way that will get rid of your Plight today, right away!"

I will go along, if you need me; hopefully the wizard can come up with a plan to rescue you. I heard that he has the Power to work a miracle, and make it last. I believe that you want this matter to be solved real fast.

The fox and the bird arrived at Blizzard's; the wizard's house, while it was still early. The sun was still shiny and bright. Emma and Grace was accompanied by an old moose, a goose, and a mouse. The wizard invited the group inside, his twin brother was gone, he went for a ride, around the loop.

Fair Grace was excited, she was glad to see Blizzard's tiny face. After she began to tell him her story, the wizard told her not to worry; I Know just what to do; if you trust me, I will see you thru.

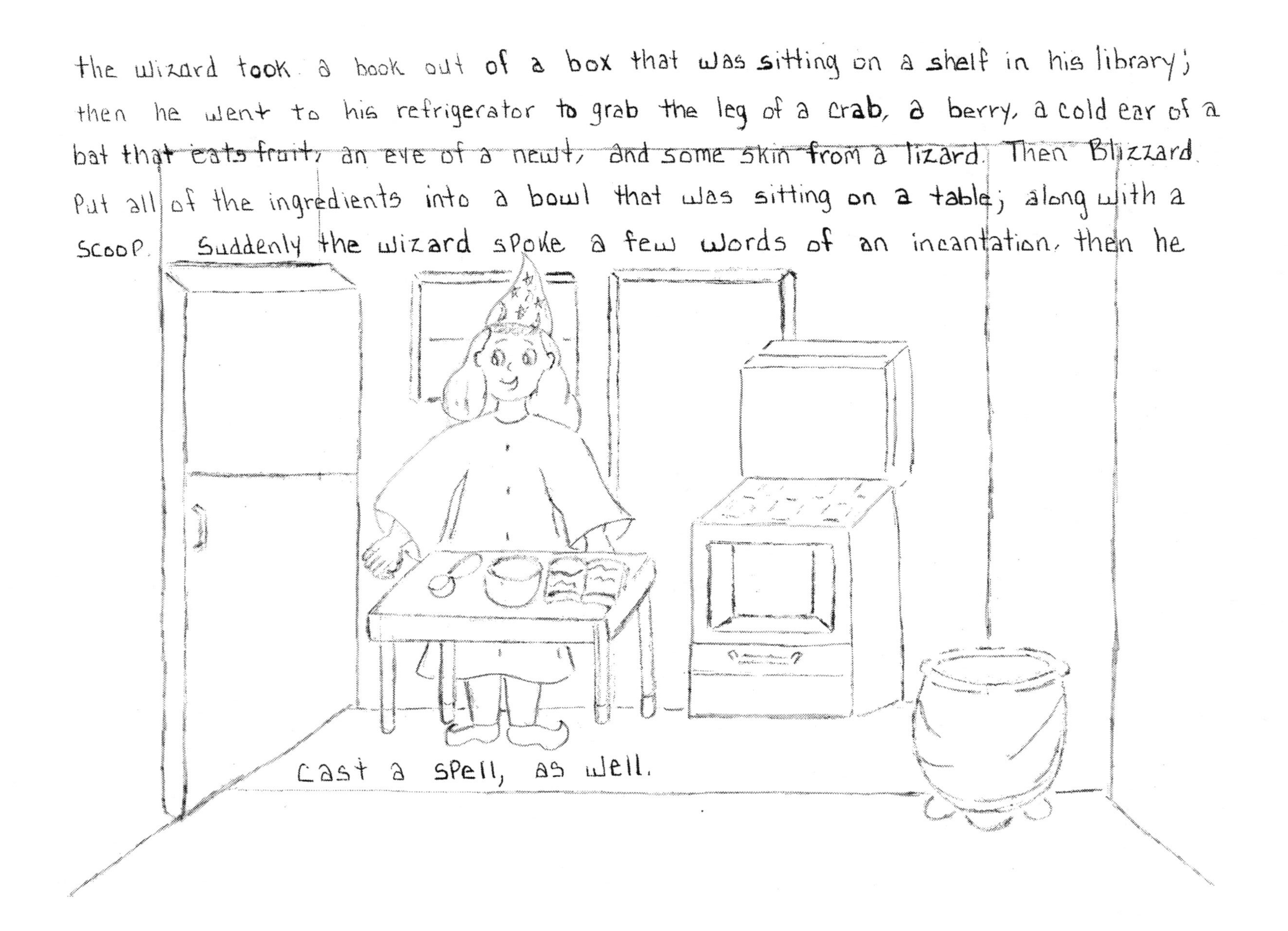
the wizard took a book out of a box that was sitting on a shelf in his library; then he went to his refrigerator to grab the leg of a crab, a berry, a cold ear of a bat that eats fruit, an eye of a newt, and some skin from a lizard. Then Blizzard Put all of the ingredients into a bowl that was sitting on a table; along with a scoop. Suddenly the wizard spoke a few words of an incantation, then he
cast a spell, as well.

Blizzard the wizard gave fair Grace a pill to take, and a glass of water to drink from a well, then he cleaned up the area that he used, because he is very concerned about sanitation, before he prepared some flat rye bread, dinner, and a cherry pie.

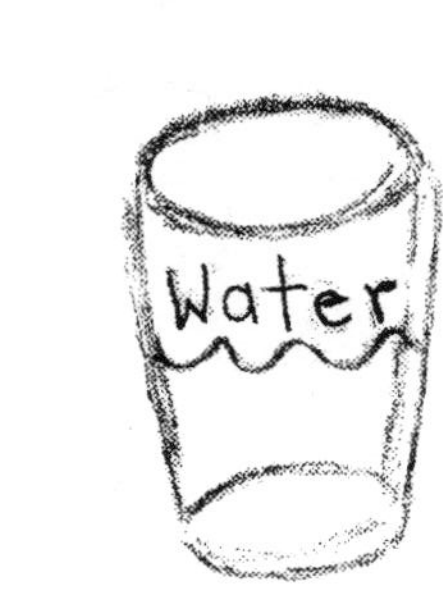

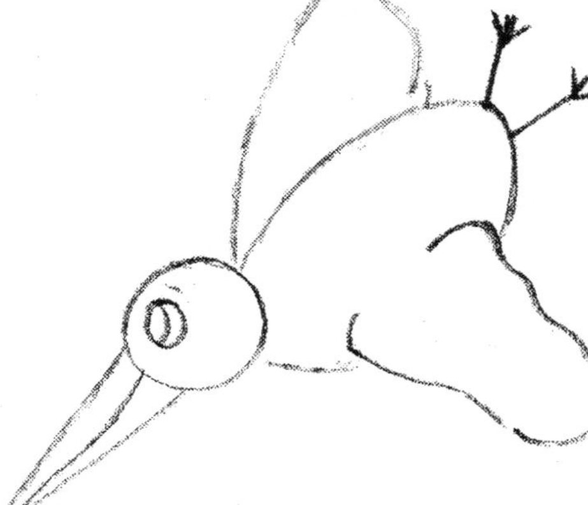

The wizard also gave the hummingbird a potion, that was poured into a bottle, it smells just like lotion, or the new rose petals of a flower, and some sage, which helps to make her voice as clear as a bell.

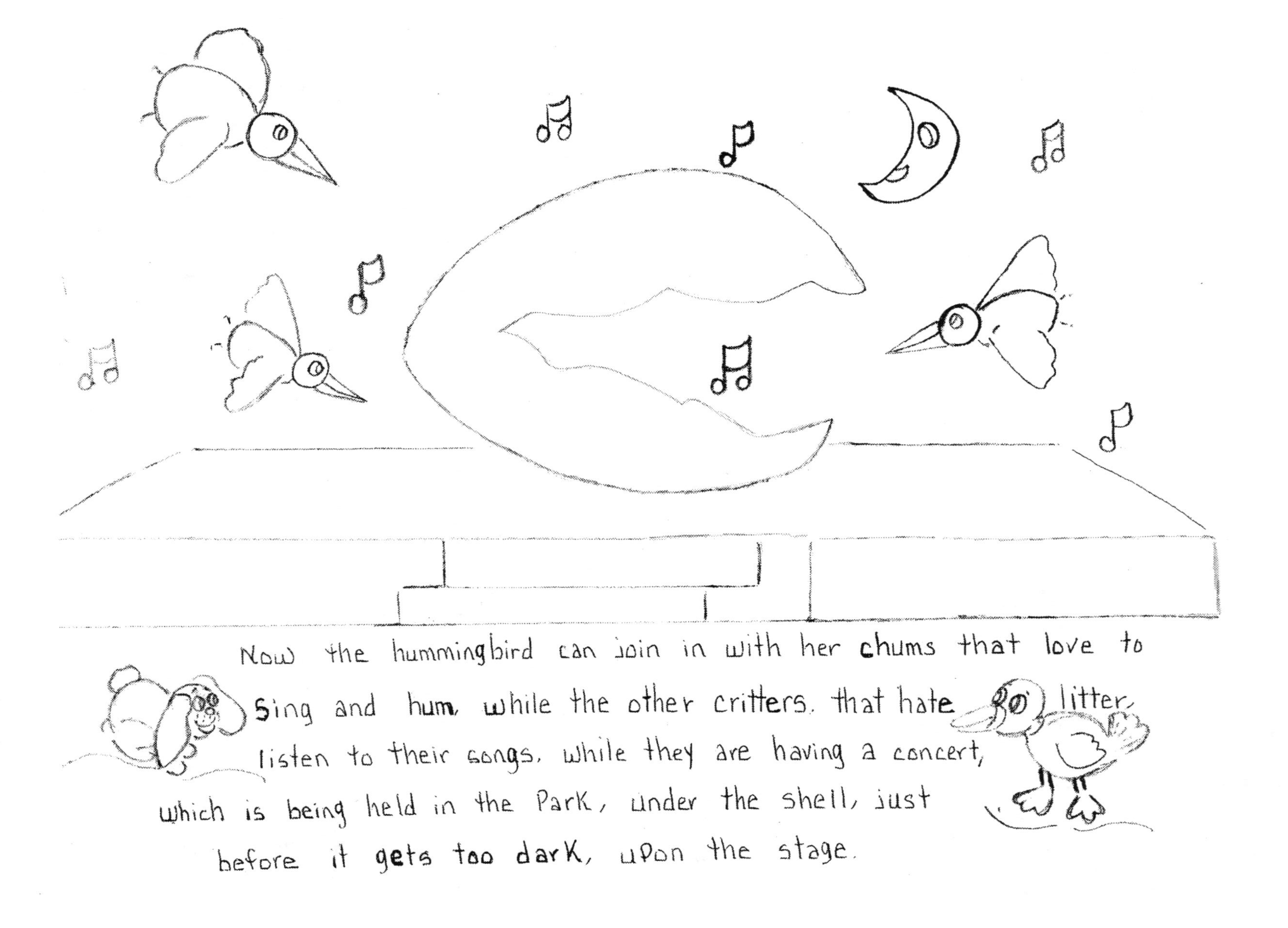
Now the hummingbird can join in with her chums that love to
Sing and hum, while the other critters. that hate litter,
listen to their songs. while they are having a concert,
which is being held in the Park, under the shell, just
before it gets too dark, upon the stage.

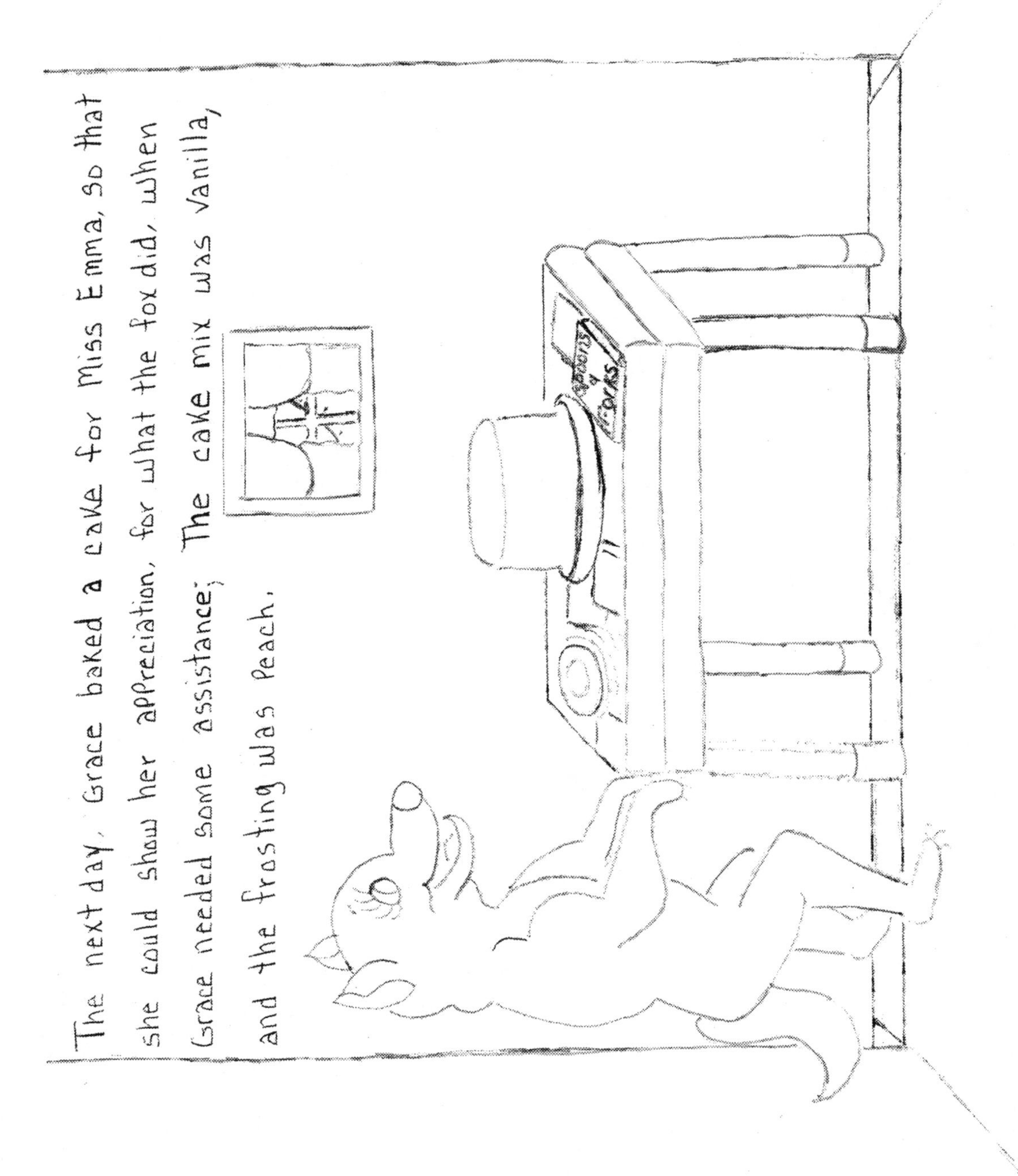
The next day, Grace baked a cake for Miss Emma, so that
she could show her appreciation, for what the fox did, when
Grace needed some assistance; The cake mix was Vanilla,
and the frosting was Peach.

The fox decided to share the goodies with every one, that resides in the woods, and then they went to the beach, so they could listen to music, and dance in the sand; some of the animals took a dip in Hoodies Lake.

Miss Emma and fair Grace asked the wizard and his brother to come
over for iced tea, later on that evening.
Blizzard and Edwin accepted the invitation; they
even took their snake along with them, and their
dog.
The snake was found hanging from a tree, and the dog's name is
Drake.

Blizzard was asked to Perform a few magic tricks, while he was spending time with his new friends. The wizard turned a dime into a stick, and a lark into a Key.

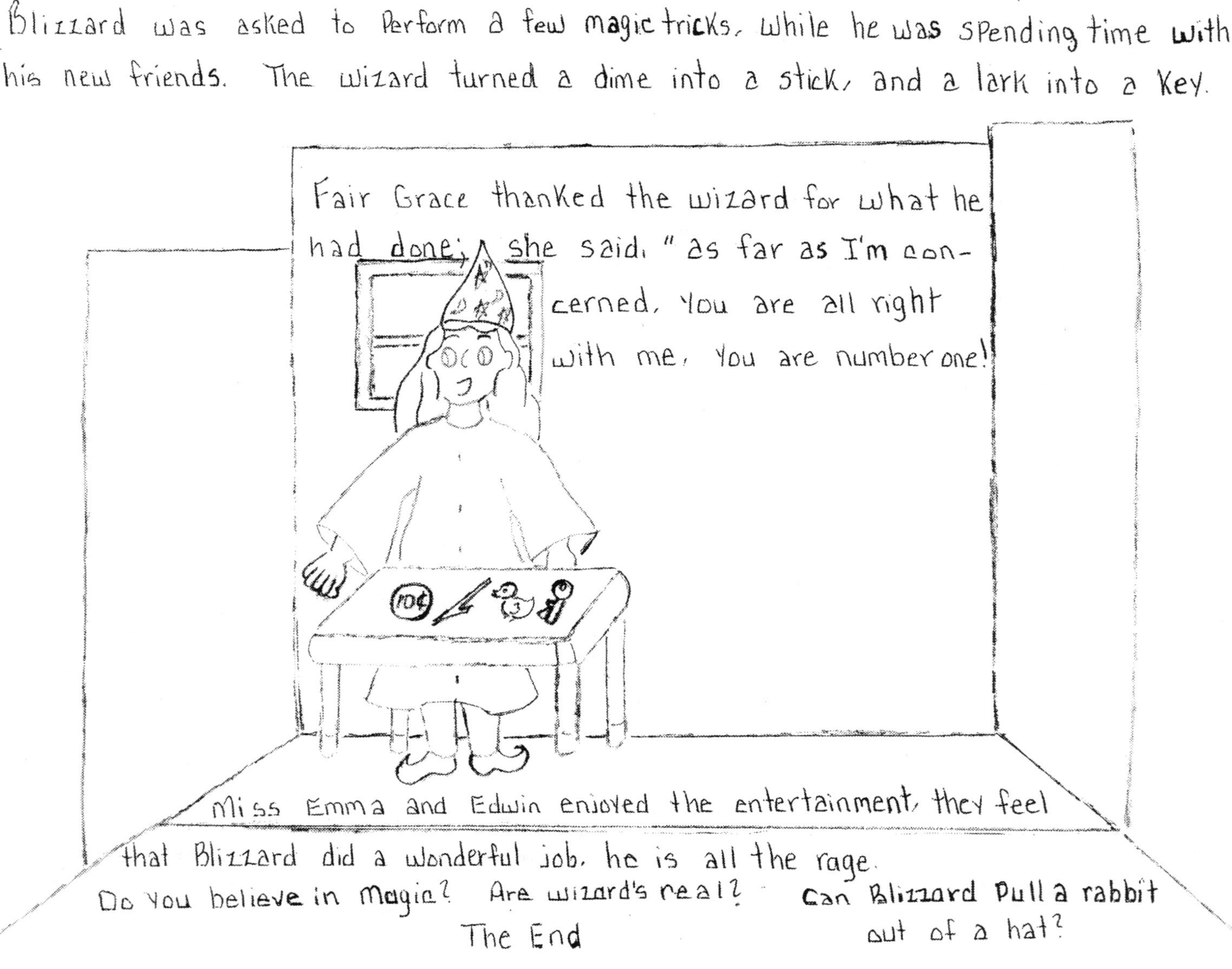

Fair Grace thanked the wizard for what he had done; she said, "as far as I'm con-cerned, You are all right with me, You are number one!
10¢
Miss Emma and Edwin enjoyed the entertainment, they feel that Blizzard did a wonderful job, he is all the rage.
Do You believe in Magic? Are wizard's real? Can Blizzard Pull a rabbit out of a hat?
The End

About the Author

She is a black woman, her name is Patricia Jean Alexander, and she currently resides in Brookfield, Wisconsin with her son, daughter-in-law, and her grandsons. She was inspired to start writing short stories for children, while she was living in Roseville, Minnesota either in 2001, or 2002. The book is compiled of at least six different manuscripts|stories about children animals or fish, it also includes the illustrations that she drew as well. She is fifty-three years old, she has a mother named Susie, a father named Roosevelt Tate, a sister named Theresa, her son's name is Fred Sr., Andrea is his wife, my grandchildren's names are Dennis, Fred Jr. Ke'erra, Alexis, Maryah, Franwuan and Sedorian.

I feel as though I have been blessed with a gift from God to inspire others to read. She decided to write stories for children, because she believes that it's a wonderful idea when parents take the time to read a bedtime story for their little ones each night, before they go to sleep. This is one way to secure the values of loves, patience, peace, joy and laughter in the home, and within the family setting so that the parents can find the special way to be drawn even closer to their special children. She loves children; and it brightens up her day, she feels better when she can put a smile on someone's face, she loves to hear the laughter of little children.